IT'S A SNOW DAY ! ! !

By :
Mickie Fosina

Illustrations by:
James Leone

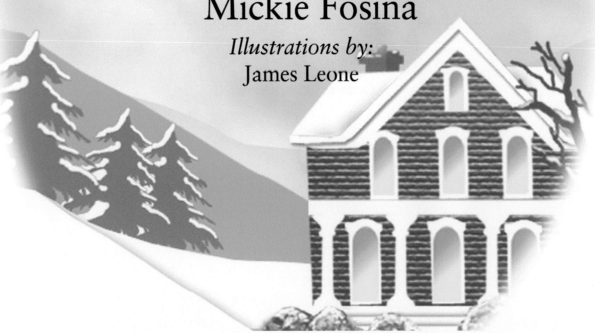

Print information available on the last page.

To order additional copies of this book, contact:
Xlibris
1-888-795-4274
www.Xlibris.com
Orders@Xlibris.com

To James Leone, the young man
whose illustrations made
my story come alive and
my dream come true.

To my niece Diane Hynes DelDuca.
You have been my inspiration
to proceed with this book.
You have donated so much
of your time to see it thru.

Matt and Mike went to bed...
Homework done and "good night" said.

During the night a storm rolled in...

Falling snow till the morning came...

IT'S A SNOW DAY!!!

Mom came in and woke the boys

"No school today"

And OH! the noise...

They jumped up and down
on the bed, until Matt fell off
and bumped his head...

It's A SNOW DAY!!!

Matt called Timmy

And Mike called Chris

What in the world do you think of this?

iT'S A SNOW DAY!!!

Mom calmed them down
and told them to eat...

You can go out and play
with boots on your feet...

IT'S A SNOW DAY!!!

It's sunny and bright and
the snow is so white...

It's a great time to have
a big snowball fight...

When they got to the park
and saw Timmy and Chris
They all gave a shout.
"What do you think about this"?

IT'S A SNOW DAY!!!

Chris had a snowball
and threw it at Mike...

that began the big snowball fight...
They laughed and laughed and
continued to play, shouting out loud

IT'S A SNOW DAY!!!

Timmy made a snowball
and rolled it big and round
till it was to hard to push,
and the boys came around...

"This is great!" said Mike to Matt

"Let's make a snowman!"
They shouted with glee.
So they rolled up some snowballs
One... Two... Three...

They picked up the snowballs,
placed one on the other
"Now we've got a snowman!"

Let's go tell mother...

"We need a hat, a scarf and a broomstick,
we'll dress him up and call him "Mick".

We need big black eyes, a bright red nose
with a pipe in his mouth and buttons for
his clothes.

They collected their supplies
and then got busy,

They laughed and played till
they were all dizzy

OH YES!

IT'S A SNOWDAY!!!

Pleased with themselves,
with something to show...

Now hungry and tired they decided to go.
It was a day - friends being friends...

Now it is time to come to an end...

It's been a wonderful...

SNOW DAY!!!

Printed in the United States
by Baker & Taylor Publisher Services